GUARDIANS OF THE GALAXY
BEST STORY EVER

TIM SEELEY
WRITER

REILLY BROWN
STORYBOARDS

IBAN COELLO & JACOPO CAMAGNI
FINISHES

JIM CHARALAMPIDIS
COLORIST

VC'S CORY PETIT
LETTERER

ARLIN ORTIZ
DIGITAL PRODUCTION

TIM SMITH 3
PRODUCTION MANAGER

JORDAN D. WHITE &
XANDER JAROWEY
CO-EDITORS

MIKE MARTS
GROUP EDITIOR

AXEL ALONSO
EDITOR IN CHIEF

JOE QUESADA
CHIEF CREATIVE OFFICER

DAN BUCKLEY
PUBLISHER

ALAN FINE
EXECUTIVE PRODUCER

ABDO
Spotlight

ABDOPUBLISHING.COM

Reinforced library bound edition published in 2016 by Spotlight,
a division of ABDO, PO Box 398166, Minneapolis, Minnesota 55439.
Spotlight produces high-quality reinforced library bound editions for
schools and libraries. Published by agreement with Marvel Characters, Inc.

Printed in the United States of America, North Mankato, Minnesota.
042015
092015

THIS BOOK CONTAINS
RECYCLED MATERIALS

marvelkids.com
© 2015 MARVEL

LIBRARY OF CONGRESS CATALOGING-IN-PUBLICATION DATA

Seeley, Tim.
  Best story ever / writer, Tim Seeley ; storyboards, Reilly Brown ; finishes,
Iban Coello & Jacopo Camagni ; colorists, Jim Charalampidis ; letterer: VC's
Cory Petit.
      pages cm
  "Guardians of the galaxy."
  "Marvel."
  Summary: "Peter Quill and Rocket recall an epic story from their jail cell.
Meanwhile, Gamora, Drax, and Groot embark on a mission to find a special
item and also break their companions out of prison"-- Provided by publisher.
  ISBN 978-1-61479-390-8
1. Graphic novels. [1. Graphic novels.] I. Title.
  PZ7.7.S424Be 2016
  741.5'973--dc23
                      2015010361

Spotlight

A Division of ABDO
abdopublishing.com

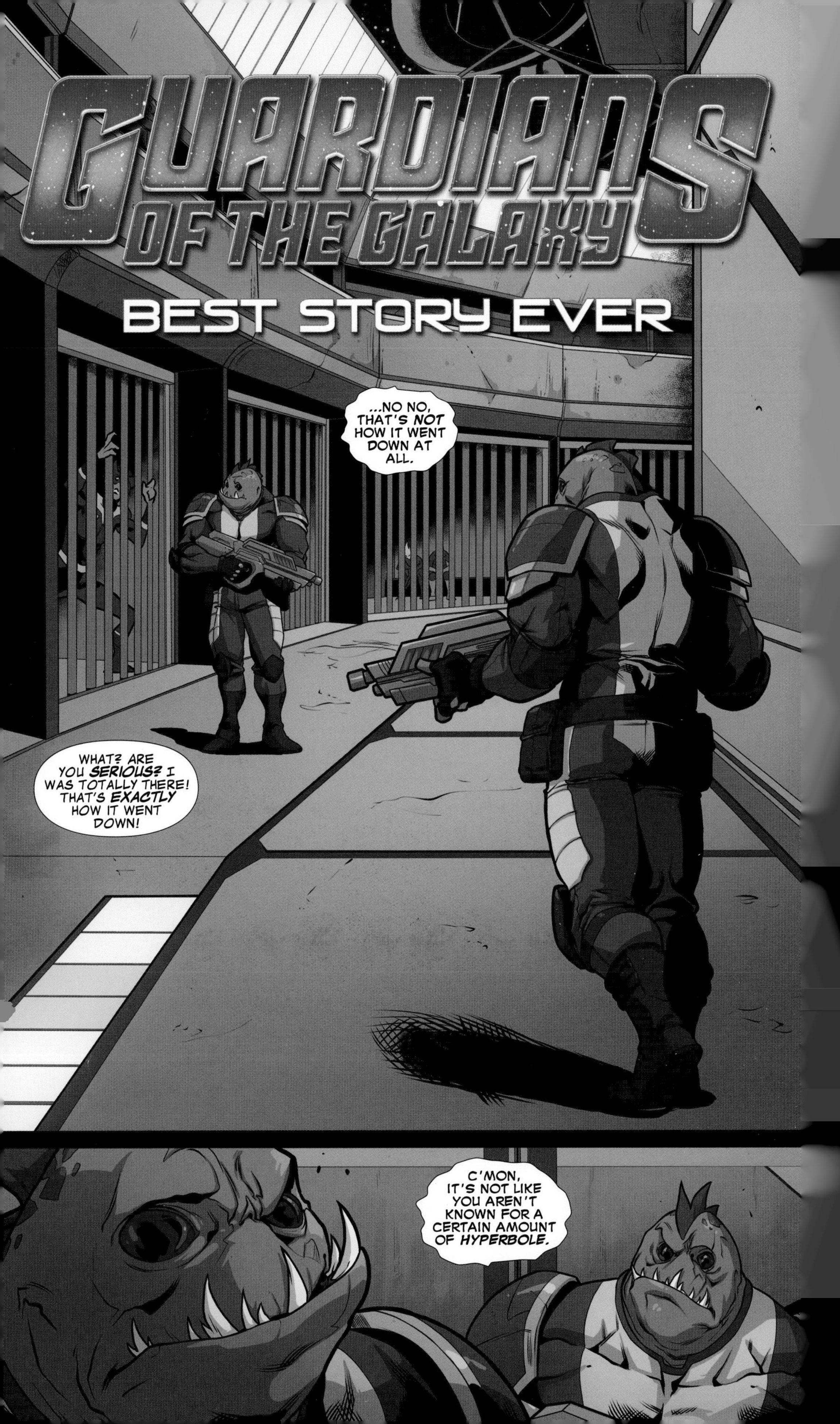
GUARDIANS OF THE GALAXY
BEST STORY EVER
...NO NO, THAT'S NOT HOW IT WENT DOWN AT ALL.
WHAT? ARE YOU SERIOUS? I WAS TOTALLY THERE! THAT'S EXACTLY HOW IT WENT DOWN!
C'MON, IT'S NOT LIKE YOU AREN'T KNOWN FOR A CERTAIN AMOUNT OF HYPERBOLE.

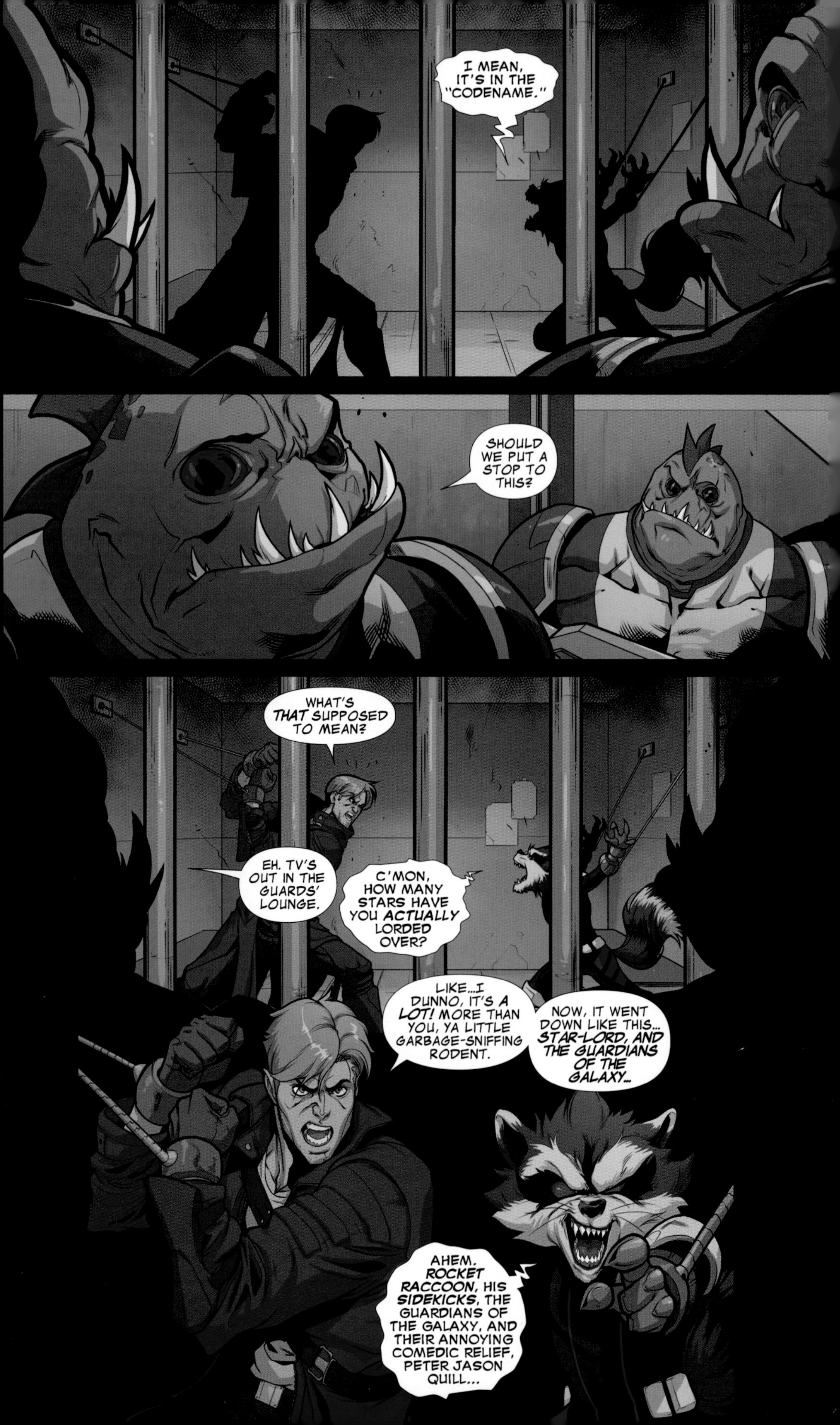
I MEAN, IT'S IN THE "CODENAME."
SHOULD WE PUT A STOP TO THIS?
WHAT'S THAT SUPPOSED TO MEAN?
EH. TV'S OUT IN THE GUARDS' LOUNGE.
C'MON, HOW MANY STARS HAVE YOU ACTUALLY LORDED OVER?
LIKE...I DUNNO, IT'S A LOT! MORE THAN YOU, YA LITTLE GARBAGE-SNIFFING RODENT.
NOW, IT WENT DOWN LIKE THIS... STAR-LORD, AND THE GUARDIANS OF THE GALAXY...
AHEM. ROCKET RACCOON, HIS SIDEKICKS, THE GUARDIANS OF THE GALAXY, AND THEIR ANNOYING COMEDIC RELIEF, PETER JASON QUILL...

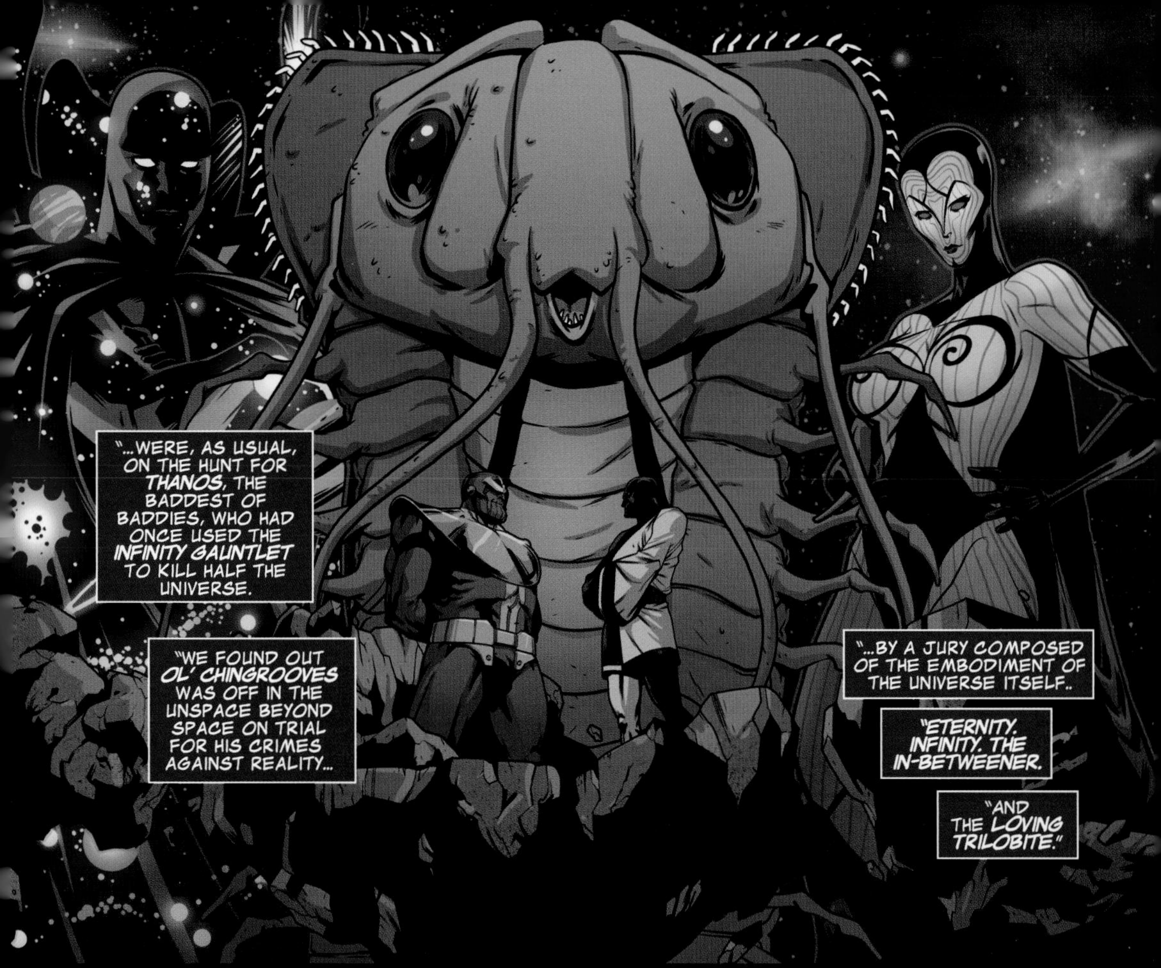
"...WERE, AS USUAL, ON THE HUNT FOR THANOS, THE BADDEST OF BADDIES, WHO HAD ONCE USED THE INFINITY GAUNTLET TO KILL HALF THE UNIVERSE.
"WE FOUND OUT OL' CHINGROOVES WAS OFF IN THE UNSPACE BEYOND SPACE ON TRIAL FOR HIS CRIMES AGAINST REALITY...
"...BY A JURY COMPOSED OF THE EMBODIMENT OF THE UNIVERSE ITSELF..
"ETERNITY. INFINITY. THE IN-BETWEENER.
"AND THE LOVING TRILOBITE."

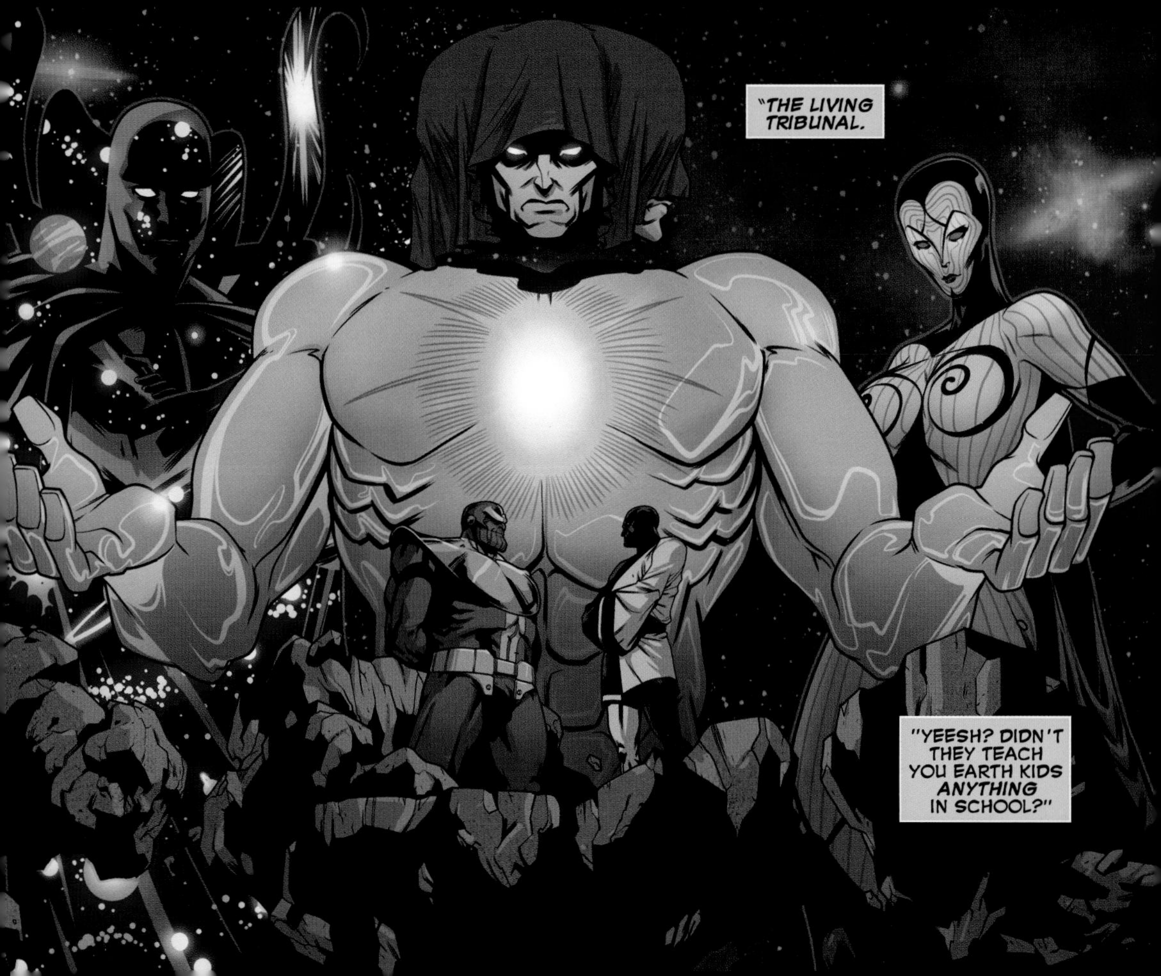
"THE LIVING TRIBUNAL.
"YEESH? DIDN'T THEY TEACH YOU EARTH KIDS ANYTHING IN SCHOOL?"

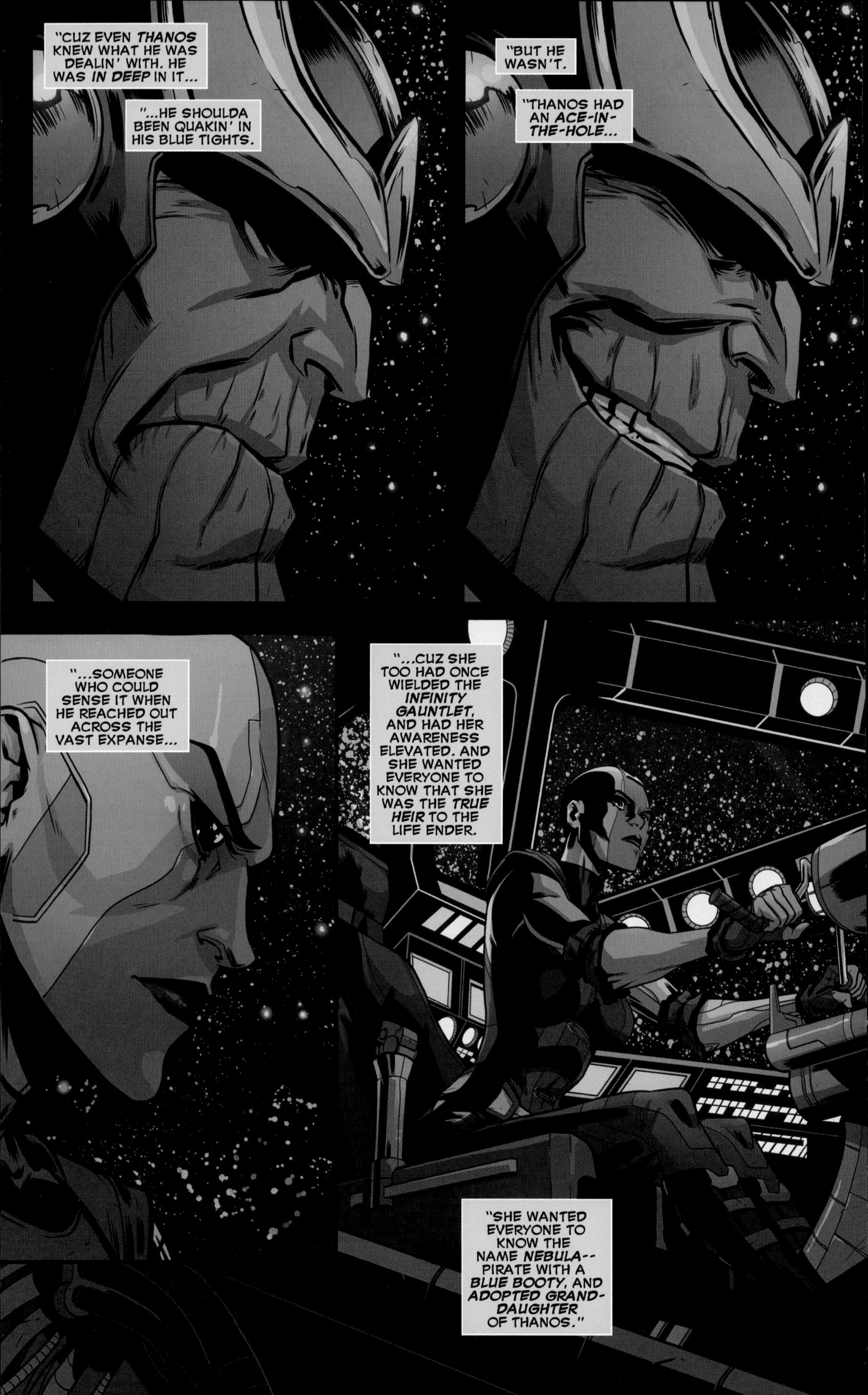
"CUZ EVEN THANOS KNEW WHAT HE WAS DEALIN' WITH. HE WAS IN DEEP IN IT...
"...HE SHOULDA BEEN QUAKIN' IN HIS BLUE TIGHTS.
"BUT HE WASN'T.
"THANOS HAD AN ACE-IN-THE-HOLE...
"...SOMEONE WHO COULD SENSE IT WHEN HE REACHED OUT ACROSS THE VAST EXPANSE...
"...CUZ SHE TOO HAD ONCE WIELDED THE INFINITY GAUNTLET, AND HAD HER AWARENESS ELEVATED. AND SHE WANTED EVERYONE TO KNOW THAT SHE WAS THE TRUE HEIR TO THE LIFE ENDER.
"SHE WANTED EVERYONE TO KNOW THE NAME NEBULA--PIRATE WITH A BLUE BOOTY, AND ADOPTED GRAND-DAUGHTER OF THANOS."

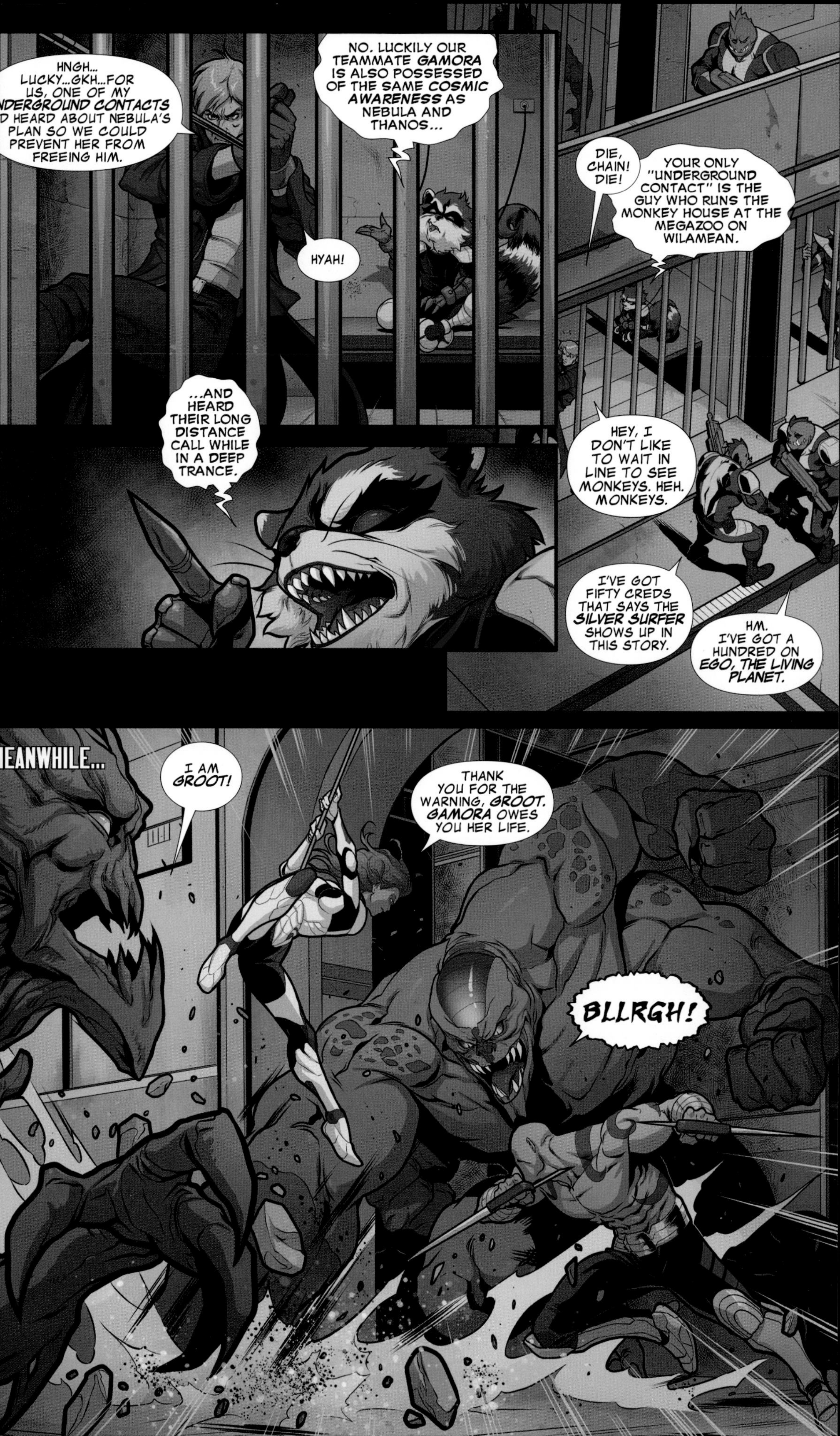

HNGH... LUCKY...GKH...FOR US, ONE OF MY UNDERGROUND CONTACTS D HEARD ABOUT NEBULA'S PLAN SO WE COULD PREVENT HER FROM FREEING HIM.
NO. LUCKILY OUR TEAMMATE GAMORA IS ALSO POSSESSED OF THE SAME COSMIC AWARENESS AS NEBULA AND THANOS...
HYAH!
...AND HEARD THEIR LONG DISTANCE CALL WHILE IN A DEEP TRANCE.
DIE, CHAIN! DIE!
YOUR ONLY "UNDERGROUND CONTACT" IS THE GUY WHO RUNS THE MONKEY HOUSE AT THE MEGAZOO ON WILAMEAN.
HEY, I DON'T LIKE TO WAIT IN LINE TO SEE MONKEYS. HEH. MONKEYS.
I'VE GOT FIFTY CREDS THAT SAYS THE SILVER SURFER SHOWS UP IN THIS STORY.
HM. I'VE GOT A HUNDRED ON EGO, THE LIVING PLANET.
IEANWHILE...
I AM GROOT!
THANK YOU FOR THE WARNING, GROOT. GAMORA OWES YOU HER LIFE.
BLLRGH!

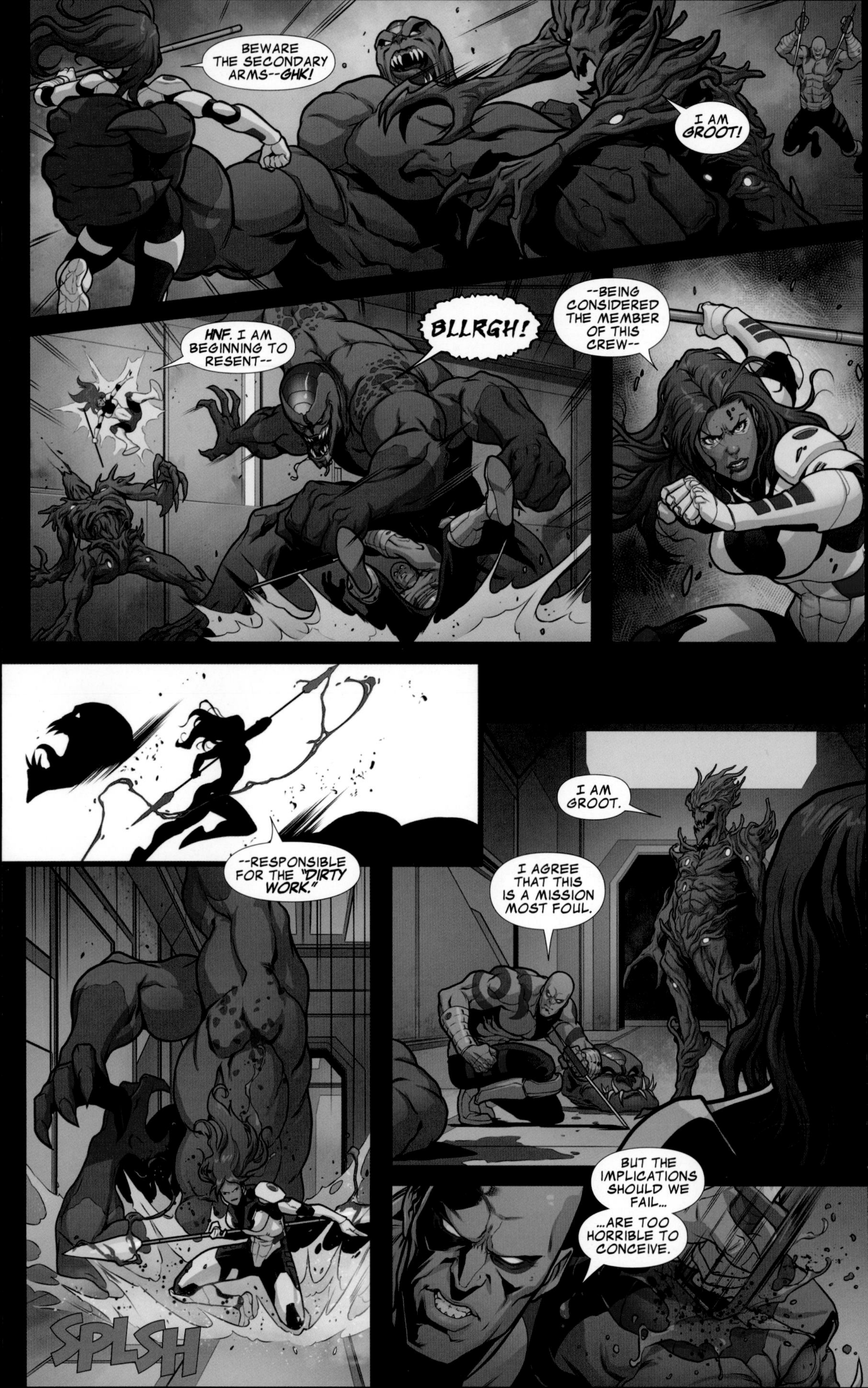
BEWARE THE SECONDARY ARMS--GHK!
I AM GROOT!
HNF. I AM BEGINNING TO RESENT--
BLLRGH!
--BEING CONSIDERED THE MEMBER OF THIS CREW--
--RESPONSIBLE FOR THE "DIRTY WORK."
SPLSH
I AM GROOT.
I AGREE THAT THIS IS A MISSION MOST FOUL.
BUT THE IMPLICATIONS SHOULD WE FAIL...
...ARE TOO HORRIBLE TO CONCEIVE.

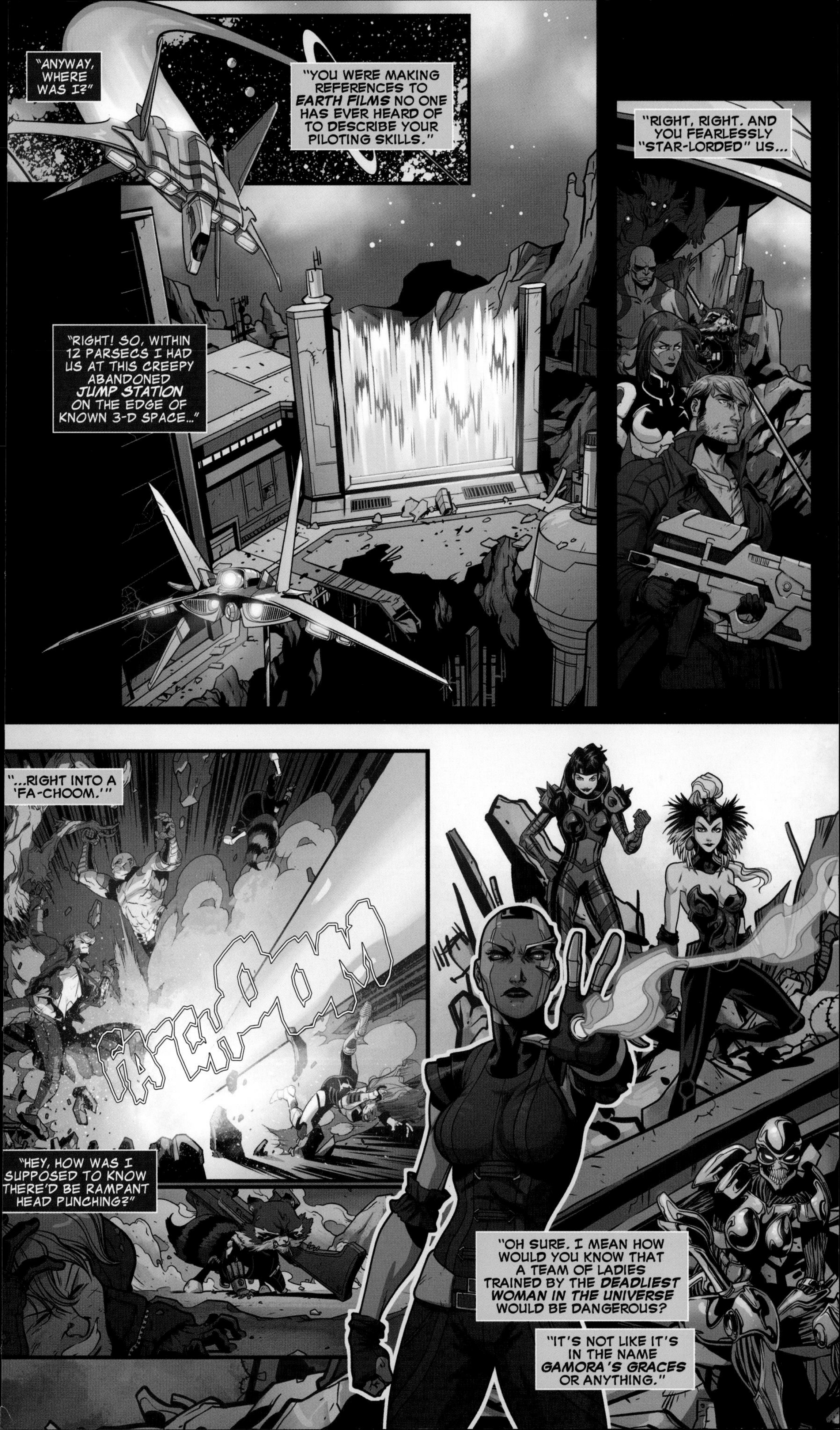
"ANYWAY, WHERE WAS I?"
"YOU WERE MAKING REFERENCES TO EARTH FILMS NO ONE HAS EVER HEARD OF TO DESCRIBE YOUR PILOTING SKILLS."
"RIGHT! SO, WITHIN 12 PARSECS I HAD US AT THIS CREEPY ABANDONED JUMP STATION ON THE EDGE OF KNOWN 3-D SPACE..."
"RIGHT, RIGHT. AND YOU FEARLESSLY "STAR-LORDED" US...
"...RIGHT INTO A 'FA-CHOOM.'"
FA-CHOOM
"HEY, HOW WAS I SUPPOSED TO KNOW THERE'D BE RAMPANT HEAD PUNCHING?"
"OH SURE. I MEAN HOW WOULD YOU KNOW THAT A TEAM OF LADIES TRAINED BY THE DEADLIEST WOMAN IN THE UNIVERSE WOULD BE DANGEROUS?
"IT'S NOT LIKE IT'S IN THE NAME GAMORA'S GRACES OR ANYTHING."

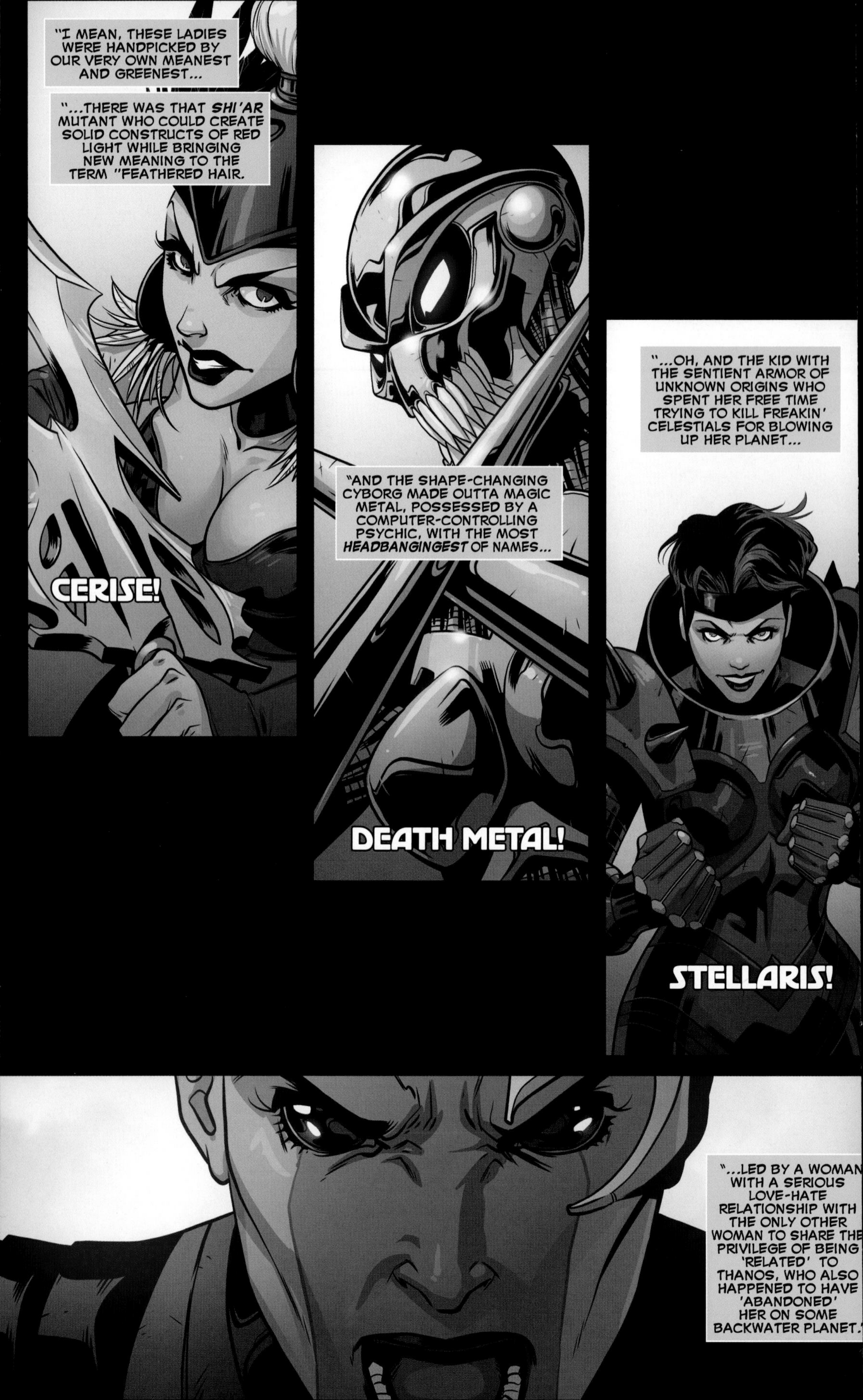
"I MEAN, THESE LADIES WERE HANDPICKED BY OUR VERY OWN MEANEST AND GREENEST...
"...THERE WAS THAT SHI'AR MUTANT WHO COULD CREATE SOLID CONSTRUCTS OF RED LIGHT WHILE BRINGING NEW MEANING TO THE TERM "FEATHERED HAIR.
CERISE!
"AND THE SHAPE-CHANGING CYBORG MADE OUTTA MAGIC METAL, POSSESSED BY A COMPUTER-CONTROLLING PSYCHIC, WITH THE MOST HEADBANGINGEST OF NAMES...
DEATH METAL!
"...OH, AND THE KID WITH THE SENTIENT ARMOR OF UNKNOWN ORIGINS WHO SPENT HER FREE TIME TRYING TO KILL FREAKIN' CELESTIALS FOR BLOWING UP HER PLANET...
STELLARIS!
"...LED BY A WOMAN WITH A SERIOUS LOVE-HATE RELATIONSHIP WITH THE ONLY OTHER WOMAN TO SHARE THE PRIVILEGE OF BEING 'RELATED' TO THANOS, WHO ALSO HAPPENED TO HAVE 'ABANDONED' HER ON SOME BACKWATER PLANET.

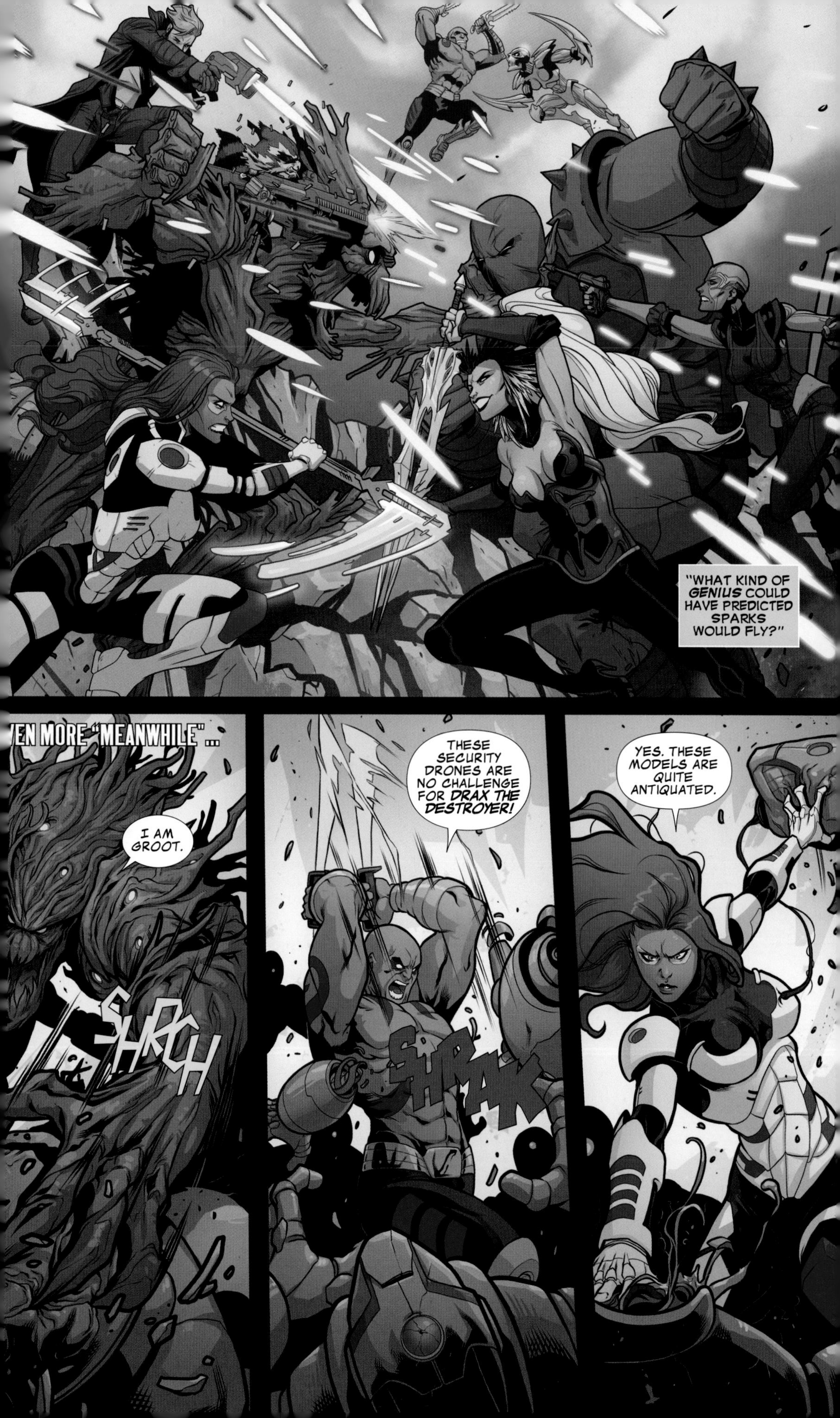
"WHAT KIND OF GENIUS COULD HAVE PREDICTED SPARKS WOULD FLY?"
VEN MORE "MEANWHILE"...
I AM GROOT.
SHRCH
THESE SECURITY DRONES ARE NO CHALLENGE FOR DRAX THE DESTROYER!
SHRAK
YES. THESE MODELS ARE QUITE ANTIQUATED.

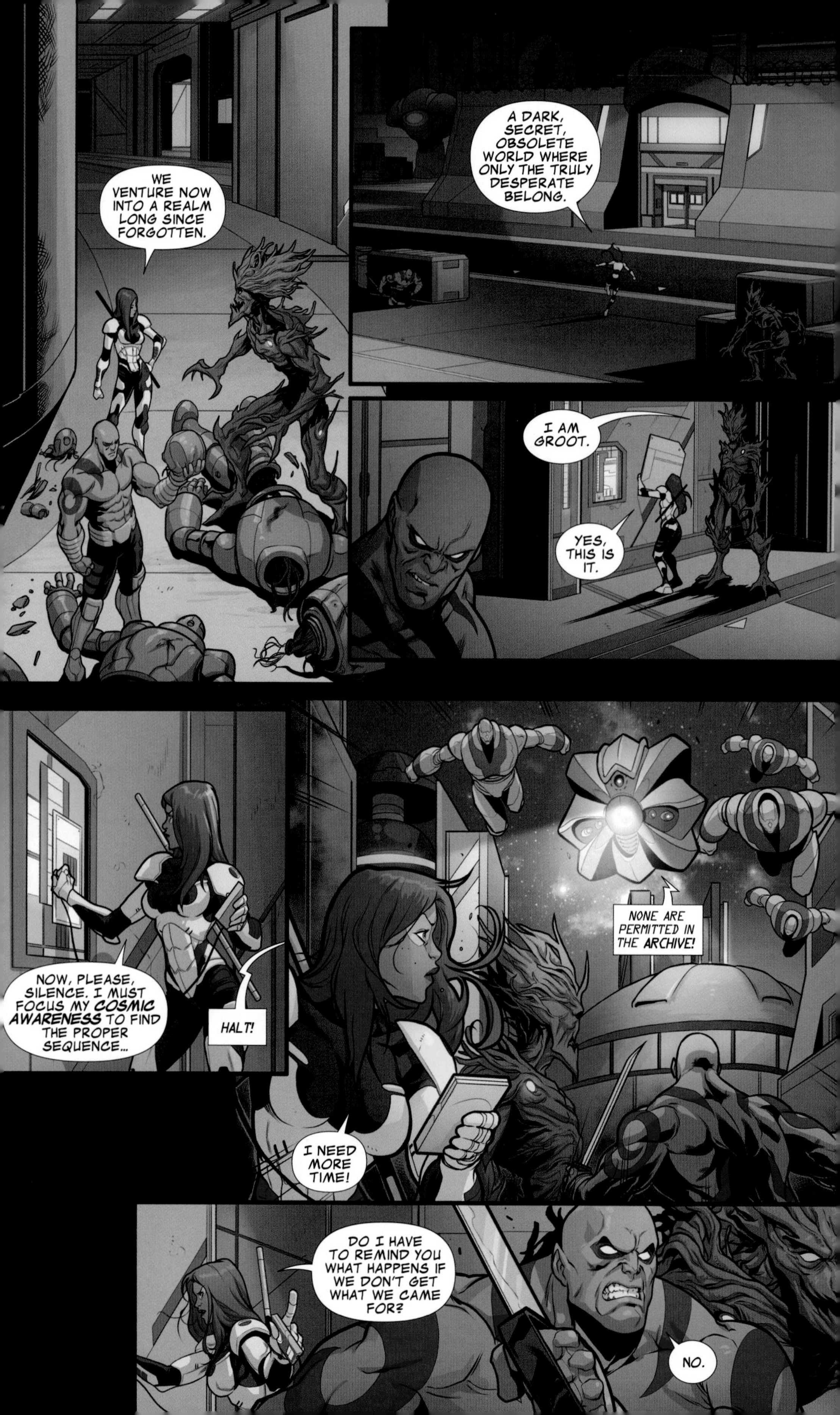
WE VENTURE NOW INTO A REALM LONG SINCE FORGOTTEN.
A DARK, SECRET, OBSOLETE WORLD WHERE ONLY THE TRULY DESPERATE BELONG.
I AM GROOT.
YES, THIS IS IT.
NOW, PLEASE, SILENCE. I MUST FOCUS MY COSMIC AWARENESS TO FIND THE PROPER SEQUENCE...
HALT!
NONE ARE PERMITTED IN THE ARCHIVE!
I NEED MORE TIME!
DO I HAVE TO REMIND YOU WHAT HAPPENS IF WE DON'T GET WHAT WE CAME FOR?
NO.

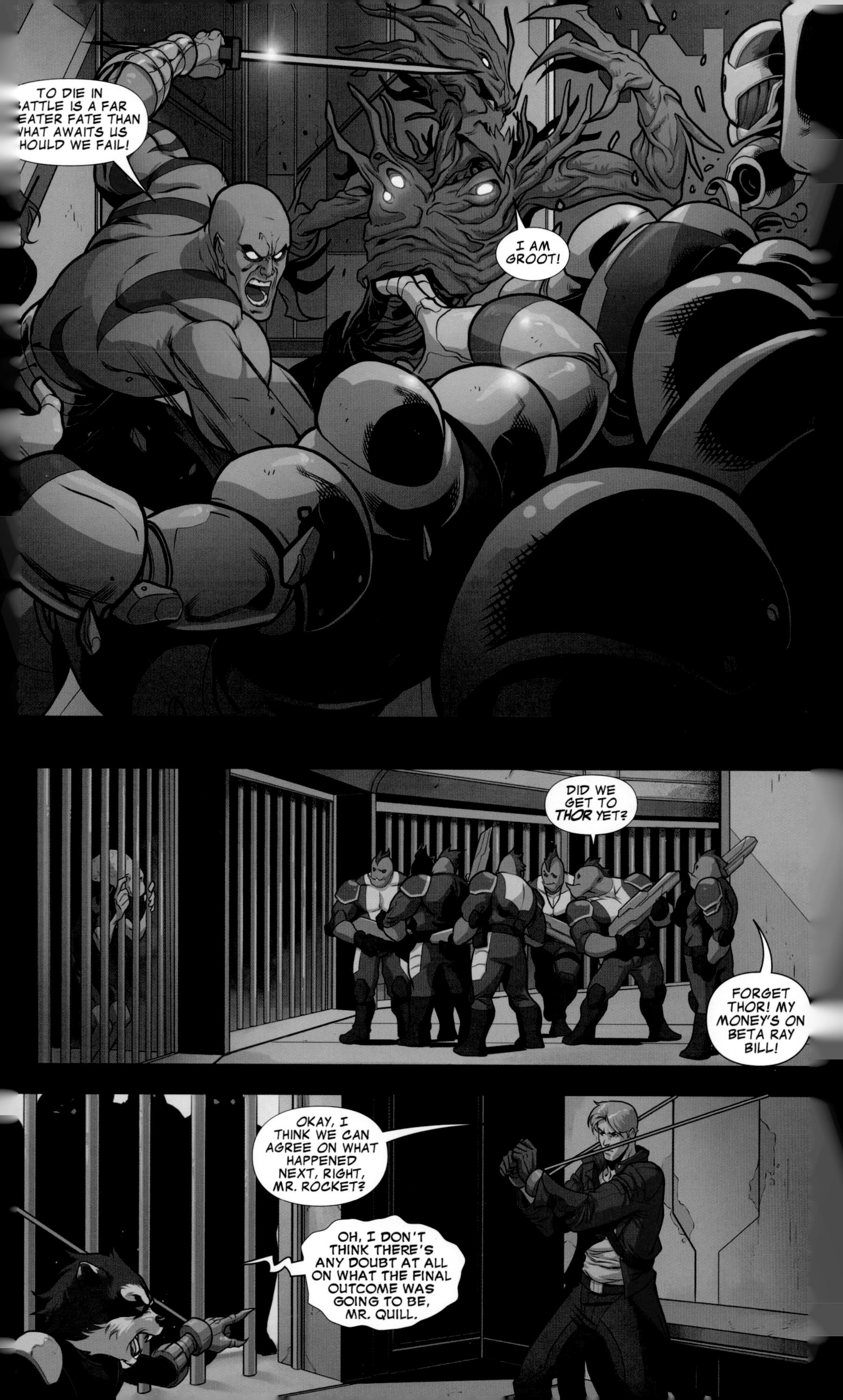
TO DIE IN ATTLE IS A FAR EATER FATE THAN HAT AWAITS US HOULD WE FAIL!
I AM GROOT!
DID WE GET TO THOR YET?
FORGET THOR! MY MONEY'S ON BETA RAY BILL!
OKAY, I THINK WE CAN AGREE ON WHAT HAPPENED NEXT, RIGHT, MR. ROCKET?
OH, I DON'T THINK THERE'S ANY DOUBT AT ALL ON WHAT THE FINAL OUTCOME WAS GOING TO BE, MR. QUILL.

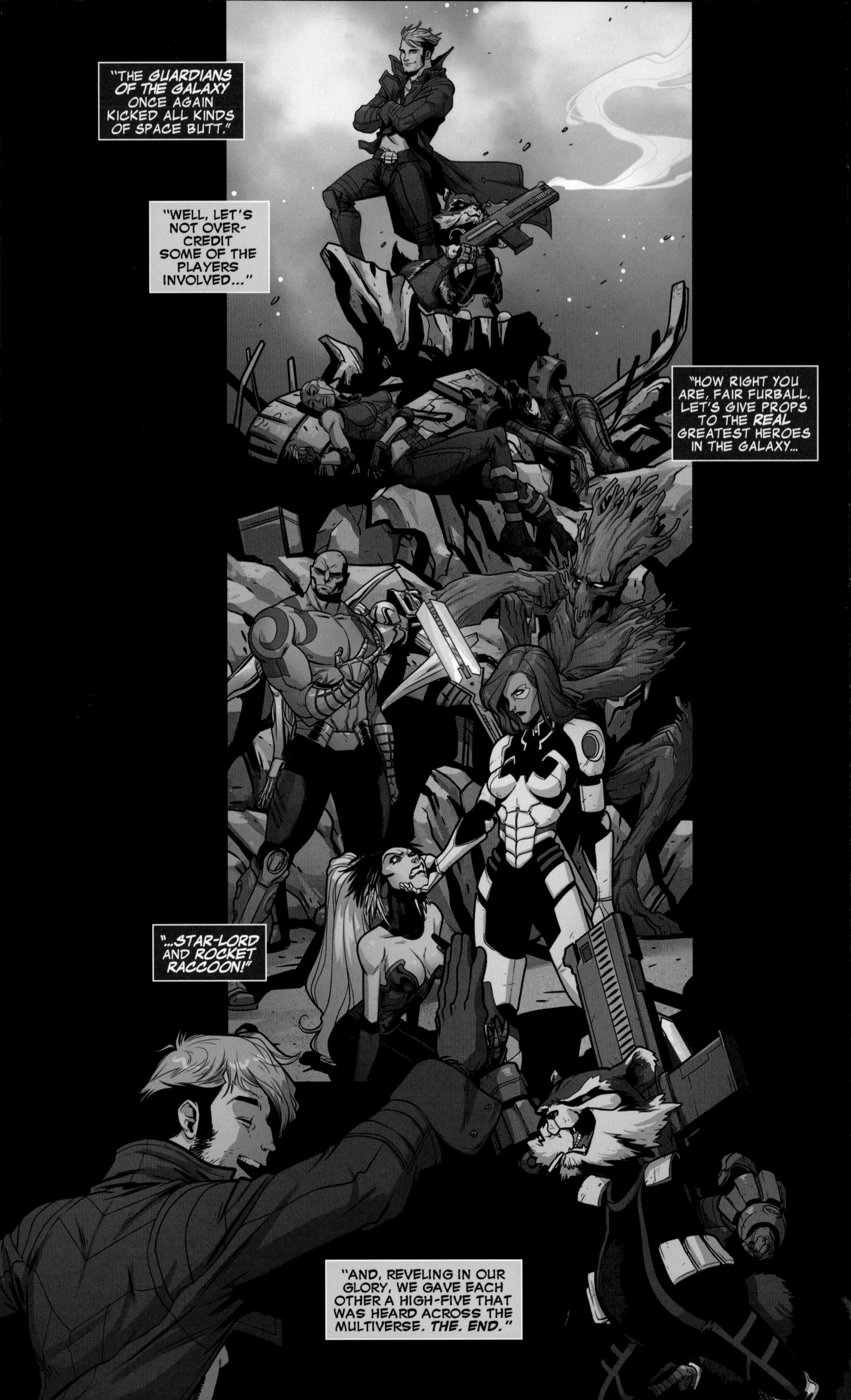
"THE GUARDIANS OF THE GALAXY ONCE AGAIN KICKED ALL KINDS OF SPACE BUTT."
"WELL, LET'S NOT OVER-CREDIT SOME OF THE PLAYERS INVOLVED..."
"HOW RIGHT YOU ARE, FAIR FURBALL. LET'S GIVE PROPS TO THE REAL GREATEST HEROES IN THE GALAXY...
"...STAR-LORD AND ROCKET RACCOON!"
"AND, REVELING IN OUR GLORY, WE GAVE EACH OTHER A HIGH-FIVE THAT WAS HEARD ACROSS THE MULTIVERSE. THE. END."

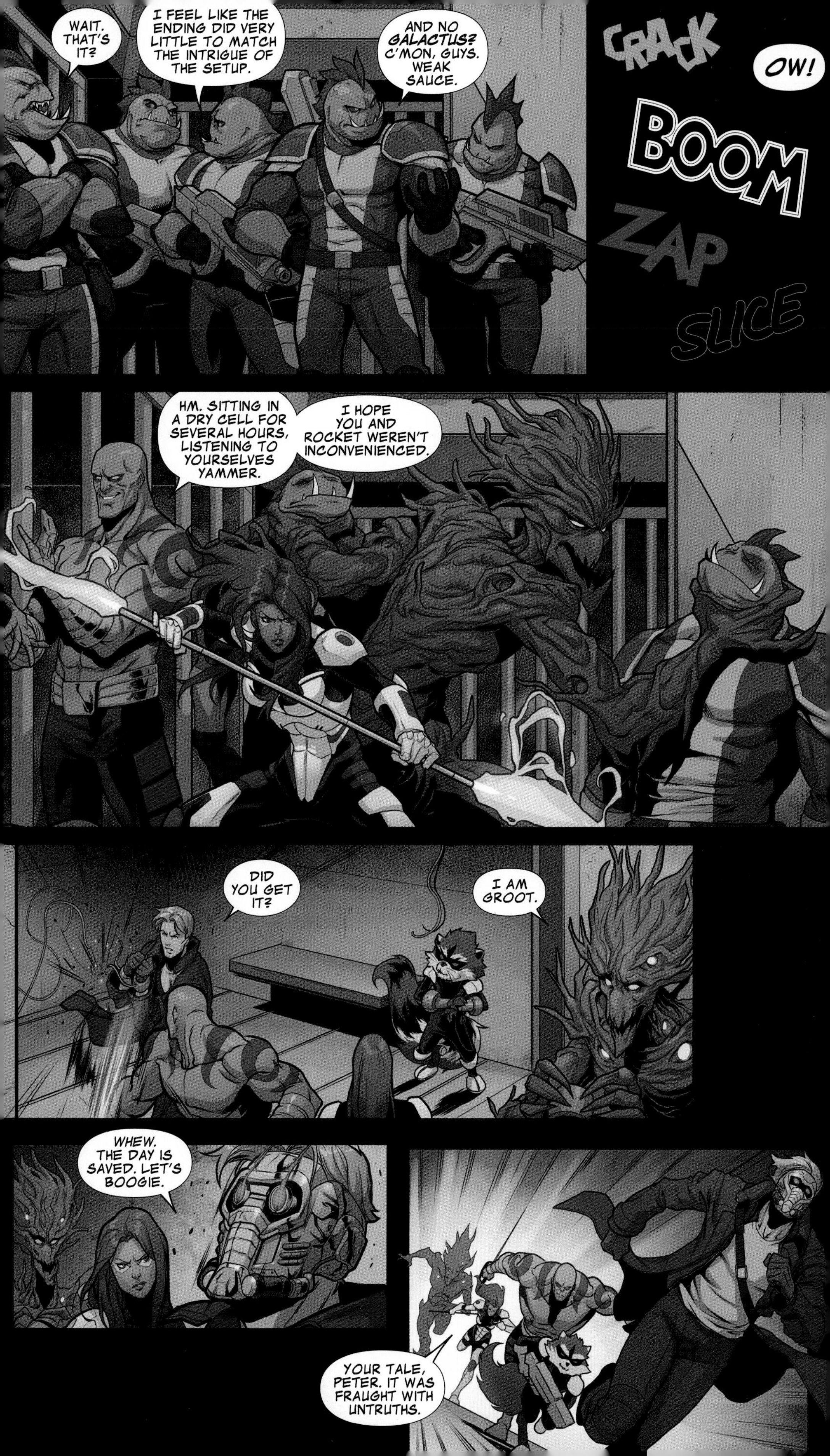
WAIT. THAT'S IT?
I FEEL LIKE THE ENDING DID VERY LITTLE TO MATCH THE INTRIGUE OF THE SETUP.
AND NO GALACTUS? C'MON, GUYS. WEAK SAUCE.
CRACK
OW!
BOOM
ZAP
SLICE
HM. SITTING IN A DRY CELL FOR SEVERAL HOURS, LISTENING TO YOURSELVES YAMMER.
I HOPE YOU AND ROCKET WEREN'T INCONVENIENCED.
DID YOU GET IT?
I AM GROOT.
WHEW. THE DAY IS SAVED. LET'S BOOGIE.
YOUR TALE, PETER. IT WAS FRAUGHT WITH UNTRUTHS.

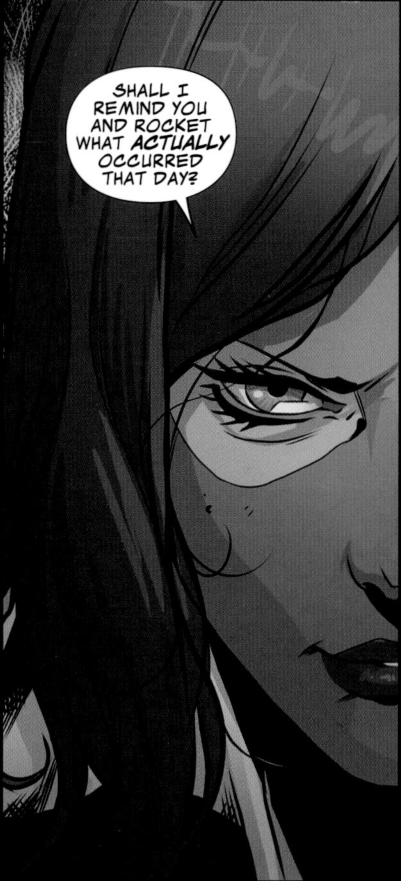
SHALL I REMIND YOU AND ROCKET WHAT ACTUALLY OCCURRED THAT DAY?

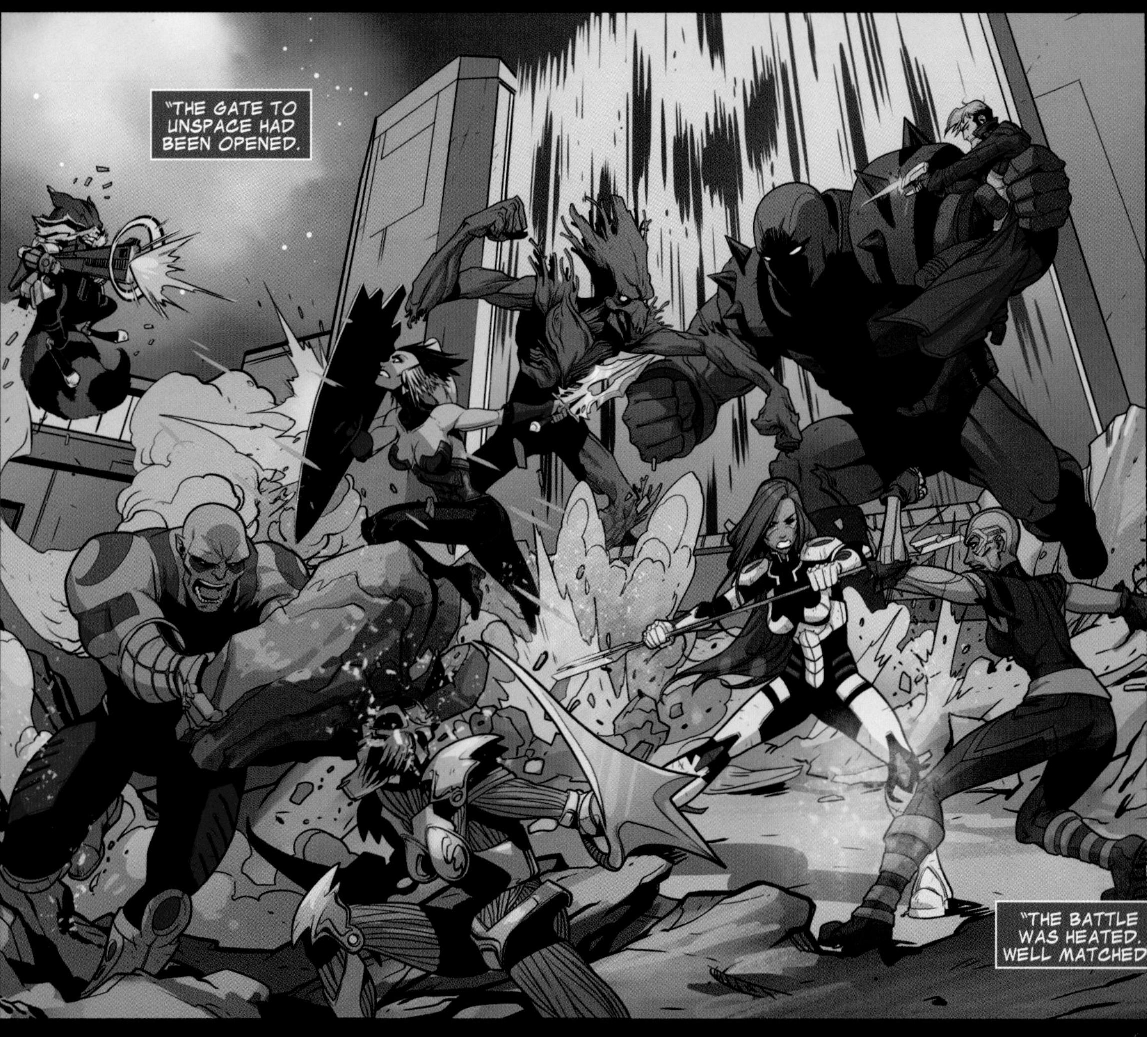
"THE GATE TO UNSPACE HAD BEEN OPENED.
"THE BATTLE WAS HEATED. WELL MATCHED.

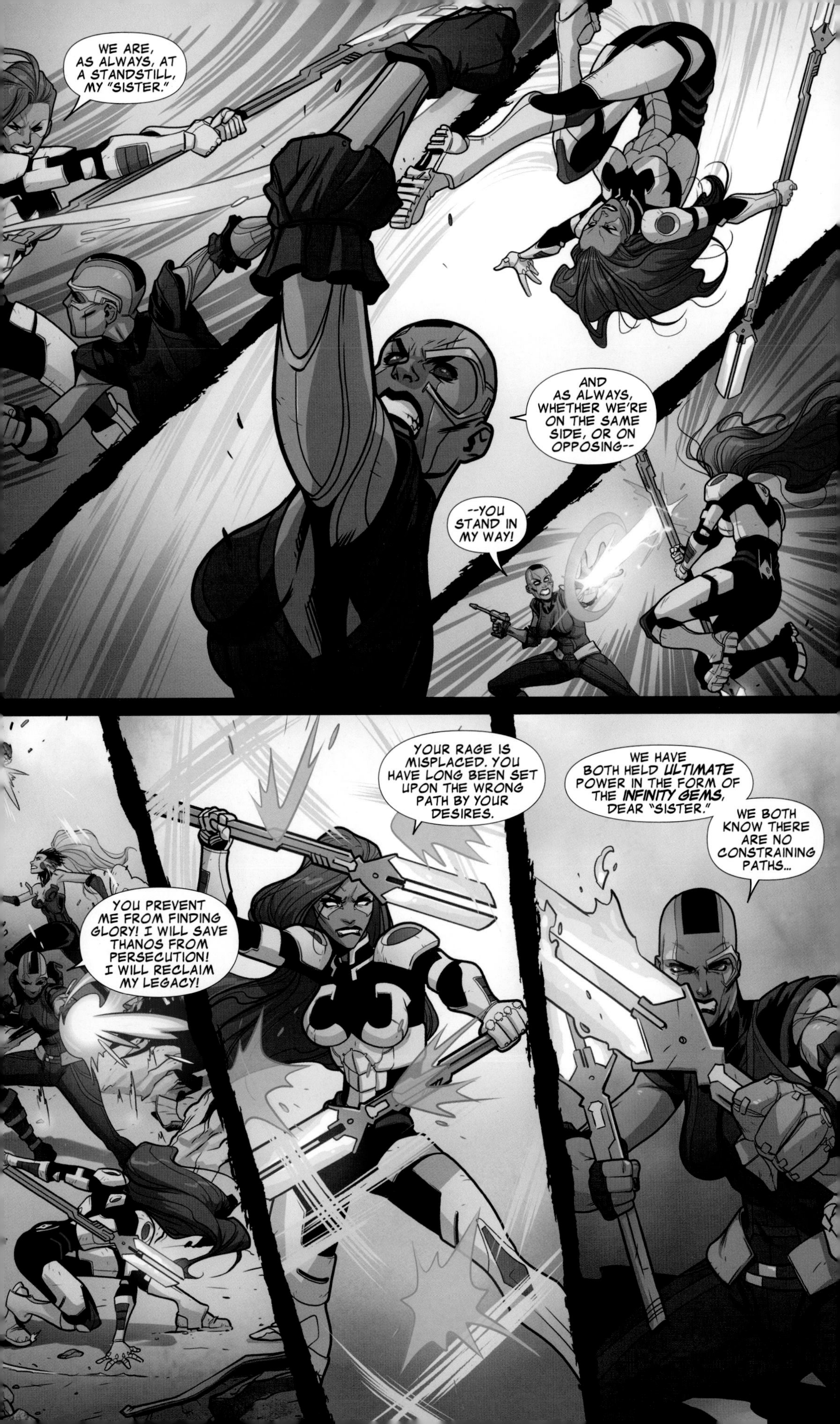
WE ARE, AS ALWAYS, AT A STANDSTILL, MY "SISTER."
AND AS ALWAYS, WHETHER WE'RE ON THE SAME SIDE, OR ON OPPOSING--
--YOU STAND IN MY WAY!
YOU PREVENT ME FROM FINDING GLORY! I WILL SAVE THANOS FROM PERSECUTION! I WILL RECLAIM MY LEGACY!
YOUR RAGE IS MISPLACED. YOU HAVE LONG BEEN SET UPON THE WRONG PATH BY YOUR DESIRES.
WE HAVE BOTH HELD ULTIMATE POWER IN THE FORM OF THE INFINITY GEMS, DEAR "SISTER."
WE BOTH KNOW THERE ARE NO CONSTRAINING PATHS...

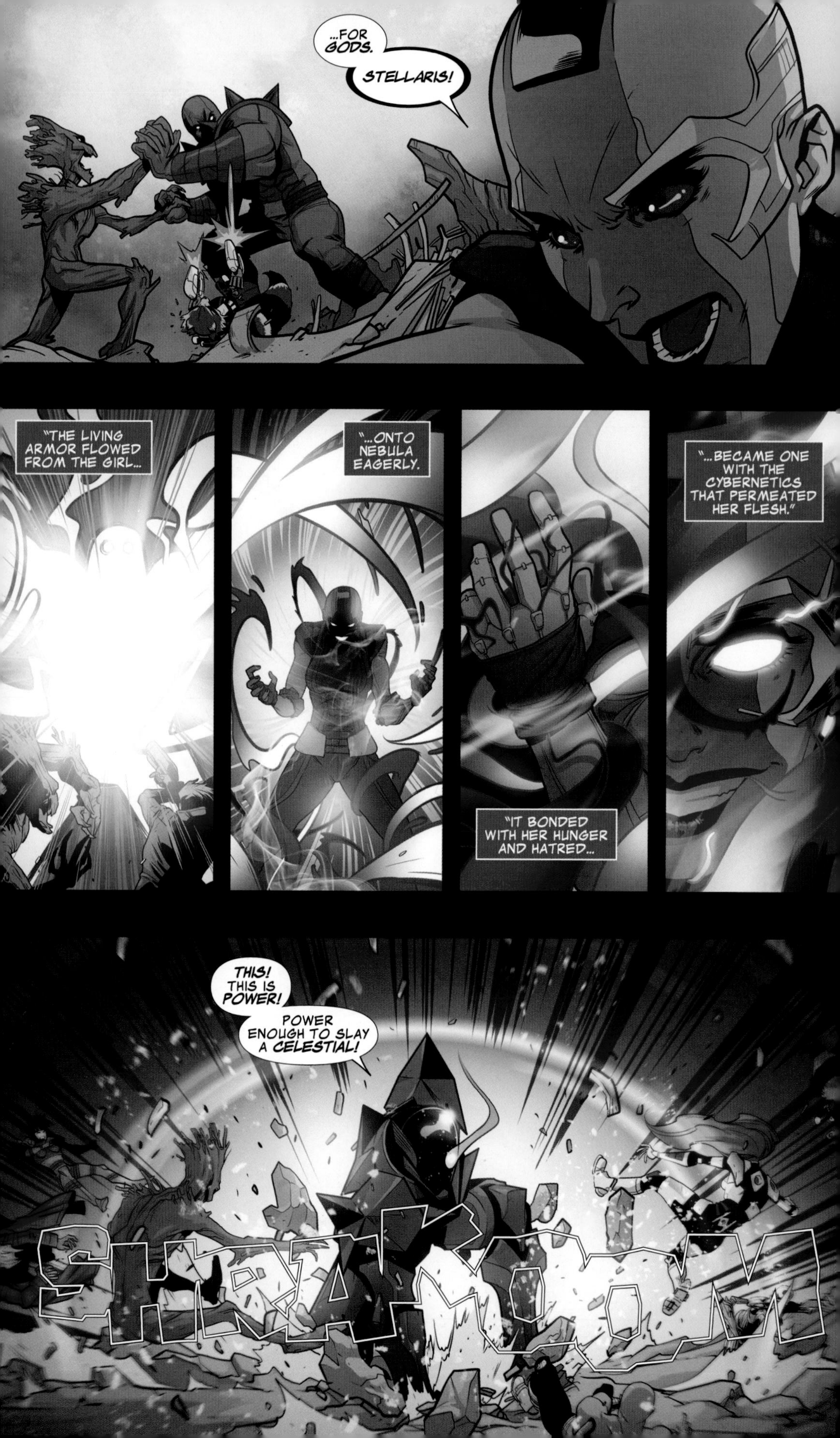

...FOR GODS.
STELLARIS!
"THE LIVING ARMOR FLOWED FROM THE GIRL...
"...ONTO NEBULA EAGERLY.
"...BECAME ONE WITH THE CYBERNETICS THAT PERMEATED HER FLESH."
"IT BONDED WITH HER HUNGER AND HATRED...
THIS! THIS IS POWER!
POWER ENOUGH TO SLAY A CELESTIAL!
SHRAKOOOM

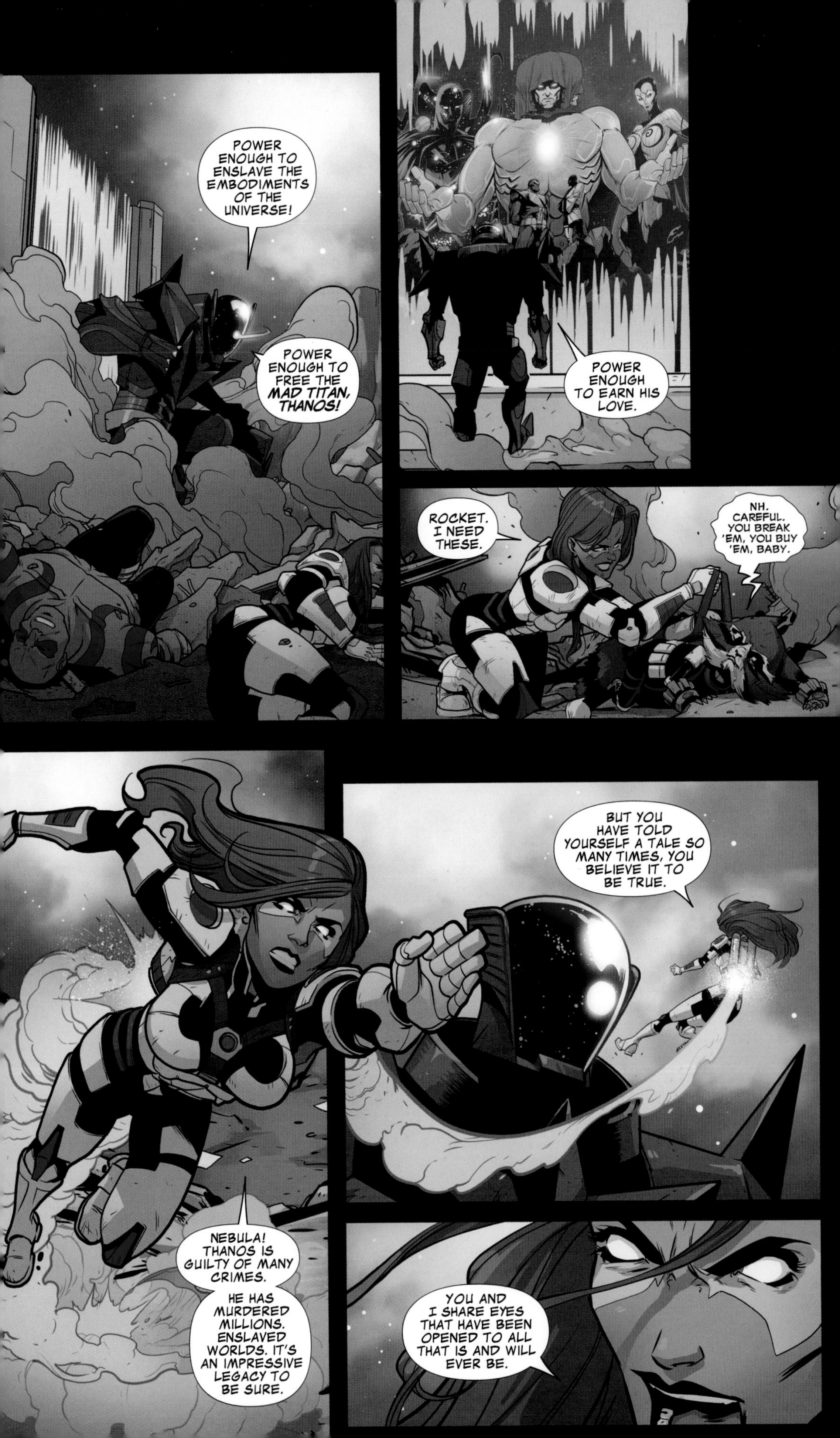
POWER ENOUGH TO ENSLAVE THE EMBODIMENTS OF THE UNIVERSE!
POWER ENOUGH TO FREE THE *MAD TITAN, THANOS!*
POWER ENOUGH TO EARN HIS LOVE.
ROCKET. I NEED THESE.
NH. CAREFUL. YOU BREAK 'EM, YOU BUY 'EM, BABY.
NEBULA! THANOS IS GUILTY OF MANY CRIMES.
HE HAS MURDERED MILLIONS. ENSLAVED WORLDS. IT'S AN IMPRESSIVE LEGACY TO BE SURE.
BUT YOU HAVE TOLD YOURSELF A TALE SO MANY TIMES, YOU BELIEVE IT TO BE TRUE.
YOU AND I SHARE EYES THAT HAVE BEEN OPENED TO ALL THAT IS AND WILL EVER BE.

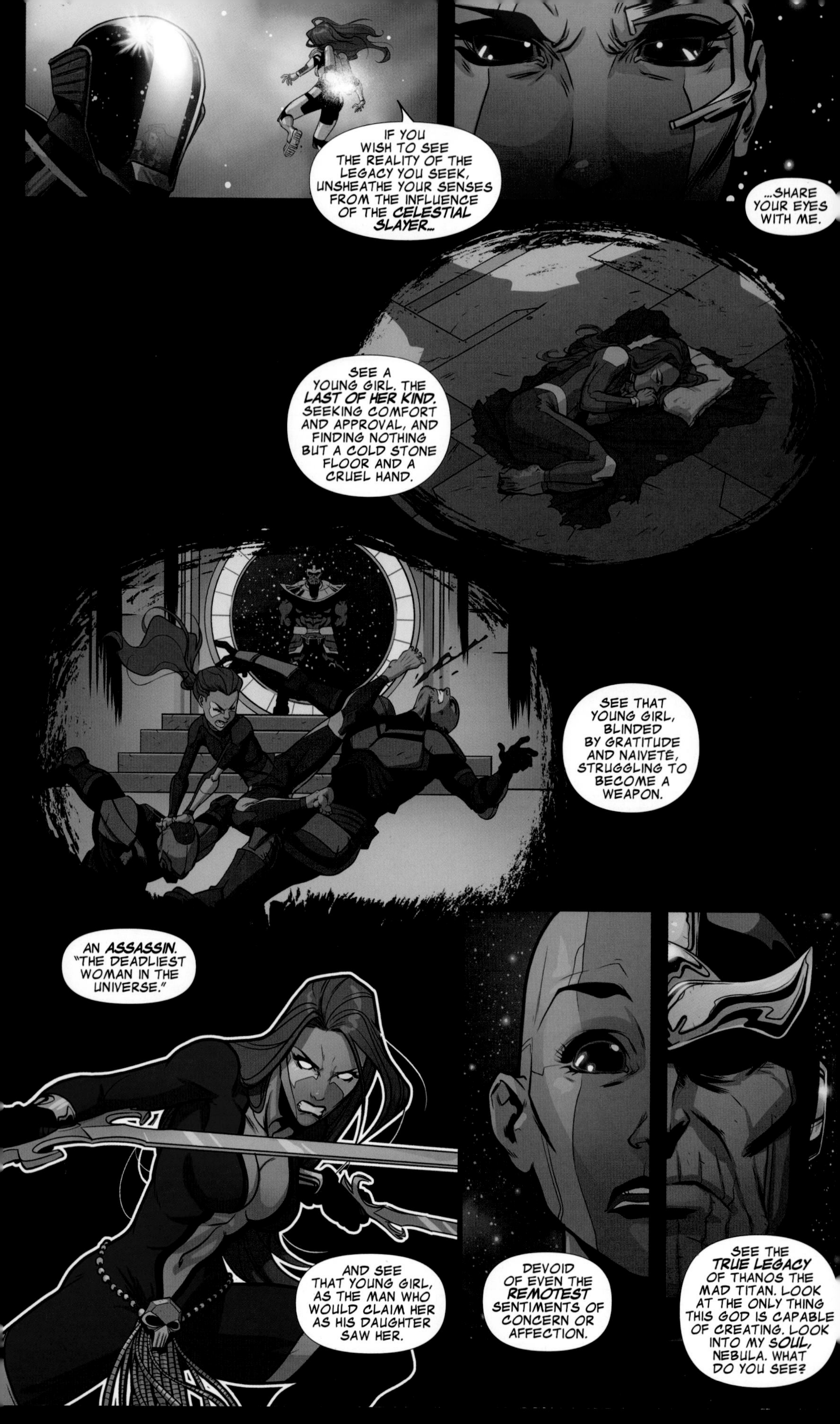
IF YOU WISH TO SEE THE REALITY OF THE LEGACY YOU SEEK, UNSHEATHE YOUR SENSES FROM THE INFLUENCE OF THE CELESTIAL SLAYER...
...SHARE YOUR EYES WITH ME.
SEE A YOUNG GIRL. THE LAST OF HER KIND. SEEKING COMFORT AND APPROVAL, AND FINDING NOTHING BUT A COLD STONE FLOOR AND A CRUEL HAND.
SEE THAT YOUNG GIRL, BLINDED BY GRATITUDE AND NAIVETE, STRUGGLING TO BECOME A WEAPON.
AN ASSASSIN. "THE DEADLIEST WOMAN IN THE UNIVERSE."
AND SEE THAT YOUNG GIRL, AS THE MAN WHO WOULD CLAIM HER AS HIS DAUGHTER SAW HER.
DEVOID OF EVEN THE REMOTEST SENTIMENTS OF CONCERN OR AFFECTION.
SEE THE TRUE LEGACY OF THANOS THE MAD TITAN. LOOK AT THE ONLY THING THIS GOD IS CAPABLE OF CREATING. LOOK INTO MY SOUL, NEBULA. WHAT DO YOU SEE?

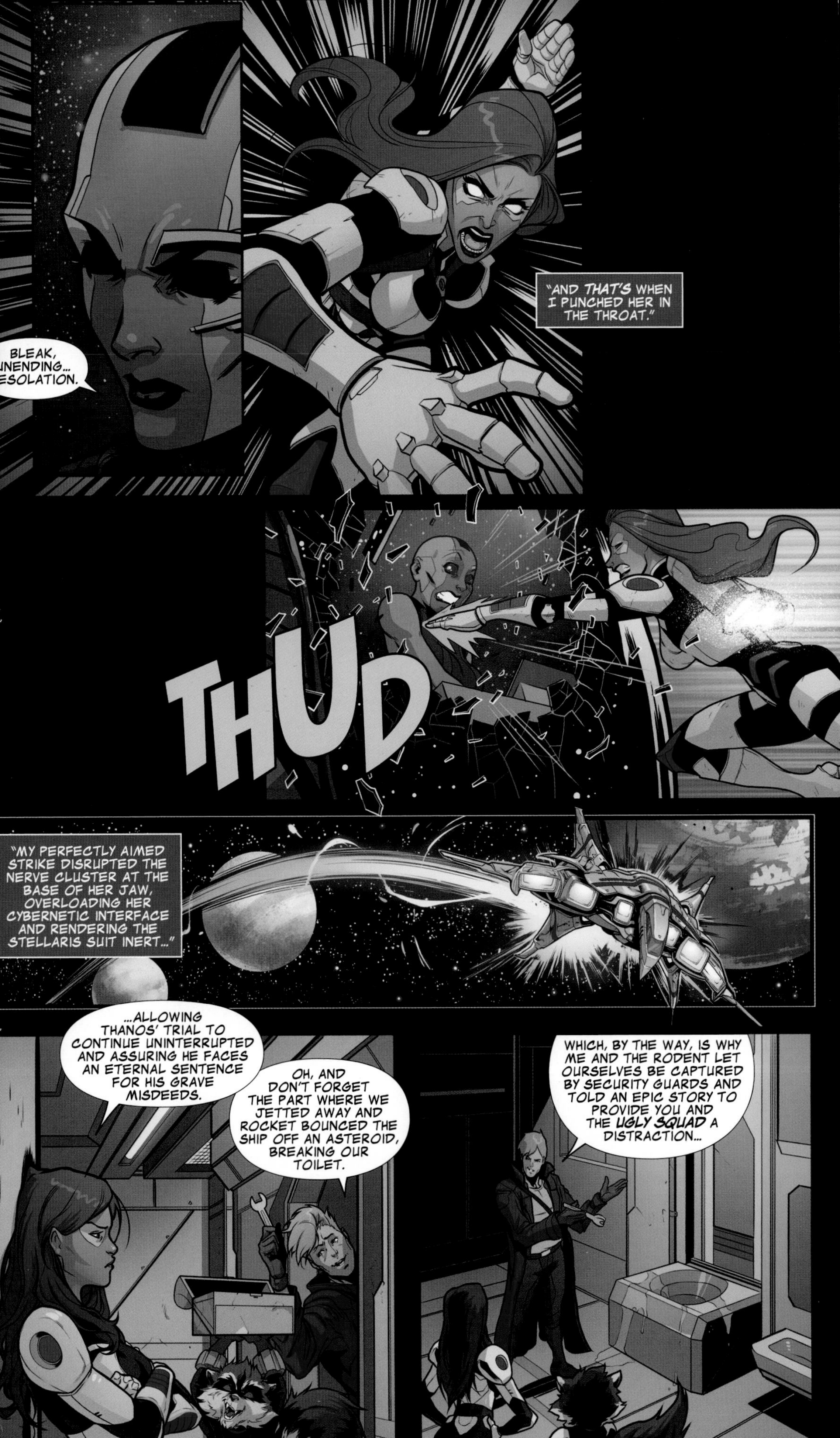
BLEAK, UNENDING... DESOLATION.
"AND THAT'S WHEN I PUNCHED HER IN THE THROAT."
THUD
"MY PERFECTLY AIMED STRIKE DISRUPTED THE NERVE CLUSTER AT THE BASE OF HER JAW, OVERLOADING HER CYBERNETIC INTERFACE AND RENDERING THE STELLARIS SUIT INERT..."
...ALLOWING THANOS' TRIAL TO CONTINUE UNINTERRUPTED AND ASSURING HE FACES AN ETERNAL SENTENCE FOR HIS GRAVE MISDEEDS.
OH, AND DON'T FORGET THE PART WHERE WE JETTED AWAY AND ROCKET BOUNCED THE SHIP OFF AN ASTEROID, BREAKING OUR TOILET.
WHICH, BY THE WAY, IS WHY ME AND THE RODENT LET OURSELVES BE CAPTURED BY SECURITY GUARDS AND TOLD AN EPIC STORY TO PROVIDE YOU AND THE UGLY SQUAD A DISTRACTION...

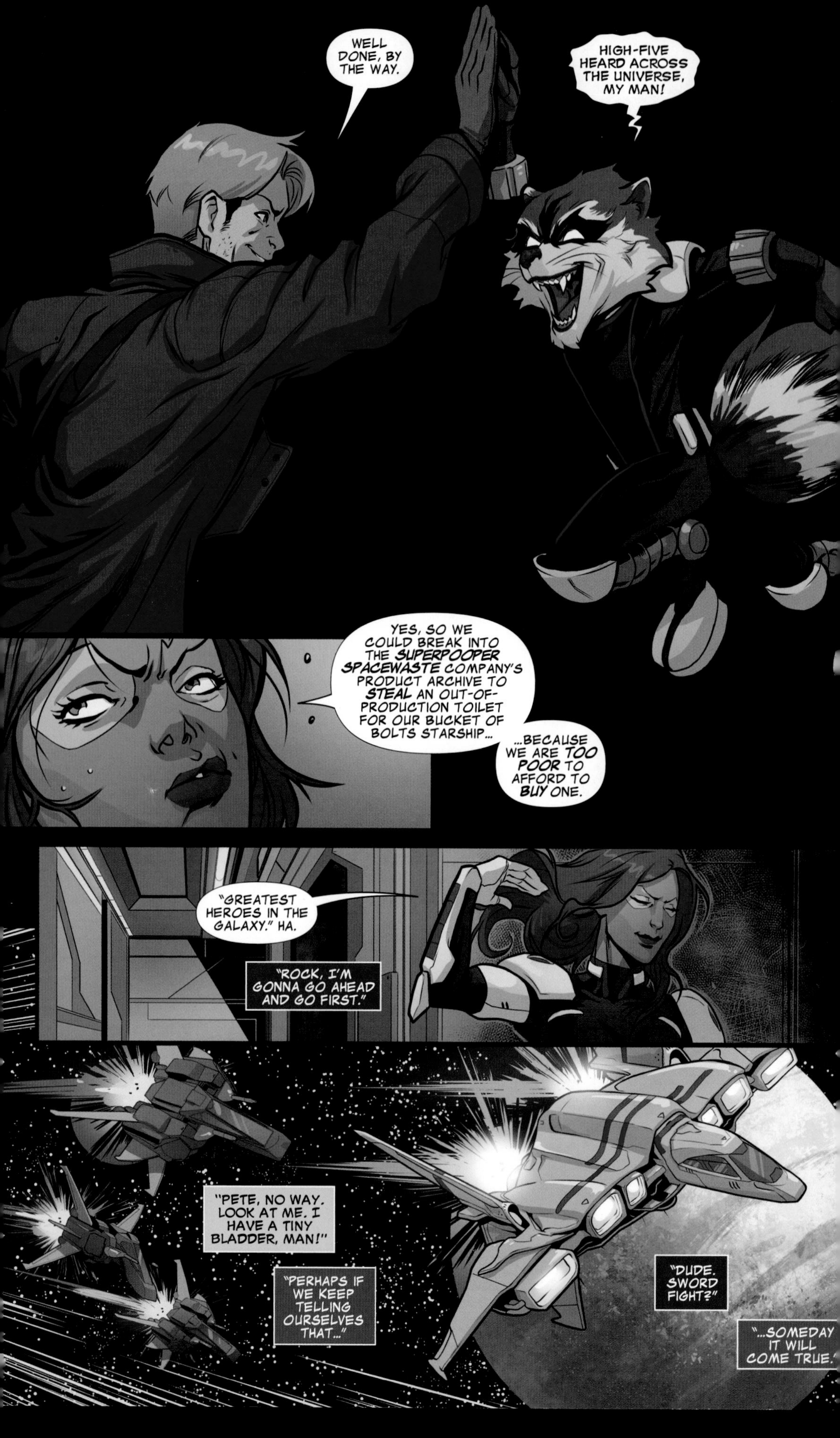
WELL DONE, BY THE WAY.
HIGH-FIVE HEARD ACROSS THE UNIVERSE, MY MAN!
YES, SO WE COULD BREAK INTO THE SUPERPOOPER SPACEWASTE COMPANY'S PRODUCT ARCHIVE TO STEAL AN OUT-OF-PRODUCTION TOILET FOR OUR BUCKET OF BOLTS STARSHIP...
...BECAUSE WE ARE TOO POOR TO AFFORD TO BUY ONE.
"GREATEST HEROES IN THE GALAXY." HA.
"ROCK, I'M GONNA GO AHEAD AND GO FIRST."
"PETE, NO WAY. LOOK AT ME. I HAVE A TINY BLADDER, MAN!"
"PERHAPS IF WE KEEP TELLING OURSELVES THAT..."
"DUDE. SWORD FIGHT?"
"...SOMEDAY IT WILL COME TRUE."

GUARDIANS OF THE GALAXY

BEST STORY EVER

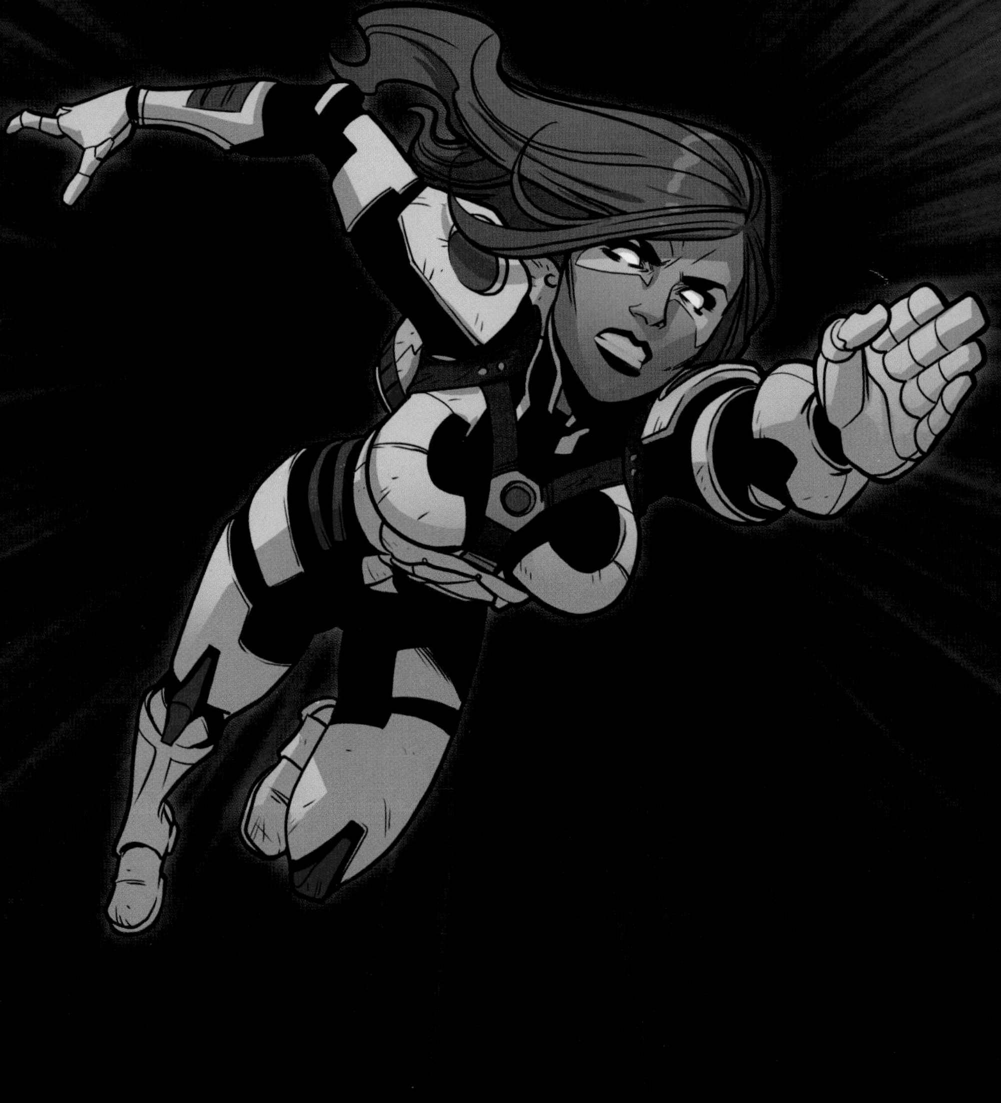

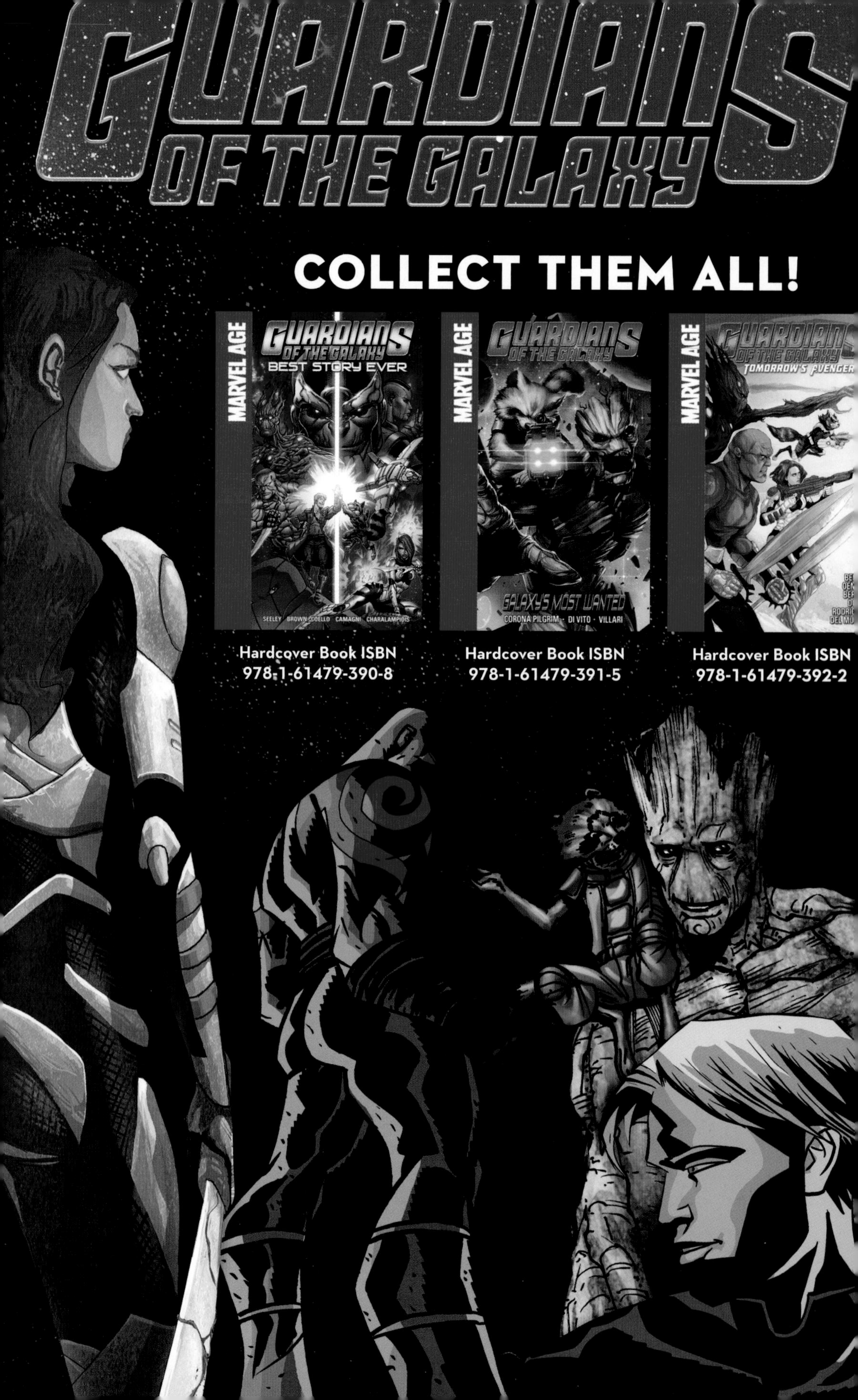

GUARDIANS OF THE GALAXY
COLLECT THEM ALL!
MARVEL AGE
GUARDIANS OF THE GALAXY
BEST STORY EVER
SEELEY · BROWN · COELLO · CAMAGNI · CHARALAMPIDIS
Hardcover Book ISBN 978-1-61479-390-8
MARVEL AGE
GUARDIANS OF THE GALAXY
GALAXY'S MOST WANTED
CORONA PILGRIM · DI VITO · VILLARI
Hardcover Book ISBN 978-1-61479-391-5
MARVEL AGE
GUARDIANS OF THE GALAXY
TOMORROW'S AVENGER
Hardcover Book ISBN 978-1-61479-392-2